THE
ADVENTURES OF
TOM
SAWYER

THE
ADVENTURES OF
TOM
SAWYER

Abridged from the original by
Mark Twain

Illustrations by
Francesca Greco

CD narrated by
Garrick Hogan

SOURCEBOOKS
Jabberwocky
AN IMPRINT OF SOURCEBOOKS

Published by Sourcebooks Jabberwocky, an imprint of Sourcebooks, Inc.
P.O. Box 4410, Naperville, Illinois 60567-4410
(630) 961-3900
Fax: (630) 961-2168
www.sourcebooks.com

Library of Congress Catalog in Publication Data
Twain, Mark
  Adventures of Tom Sawyer / Mark Twain.
    p. cm.
  Summary: An abridged version of the classic story of a mischievous 19th-century boy in a Mississippi River town and his friends, Huck Finn and Becky Thatcher, as they run away from home, witness a murder, and find treasure in a cave. Accompanying CD has narration, music, and sound effects.

[1. Adventure and adventurers--Fiction. 2. Mississippi River--Fiction. 3. Missouri--Fiction.] I. Title.

PZ7.T888Ad 2008
[Fic]--dc22
                              2007045239

                          Printed in China.
                    OGP 10 9 8 7 6 5

Source of Production: O.G. Printing Productions, Ltd. Kowloon, Hong Kong
Date of Production: August 2011
ID # 15883

TABLE OF CONTENTS

Chapter 1

TOM'S IN TROUBLE AGAIN

"Tom! Tom! What's gone with that boy, I wonder? You Tom! I never did see the beat of that boy!"

There was a slight noise behind her and she turned just in time to seize a small boy by the slack of his roundabout and arrest his flight.

"There! I might 'a' thought of that closet. What you been doing in there?"

"Nothing."

"Nothing! Look at your hands. And look at your mouth. What is that truck?"

"I don't know, aunt."

"Well, I know. It's jam, that's what it is. Forty times I've said if you didn't let that jam alone I'd skin you. Hand me that switch."

The switch hovered in the air, the peril was desperate.

"My! Look behind you, aunt!"

The old lady whirled around, and snatched her skirts out of danger and the lad fled on the instant, scrambled up the high board fence, and disappeared over it. His Aunt Polly stood surprised a moment, and then broke into a gentle laugh.

"Hang the boy, can't I ever learn anything? He'll play hookey this afternoon and I'll just be obliged to make him work, tomorrow, to punish him. It's mighty hard to make him work Saturdays, when all the boys is having a holiday, but he hates work more than he hates anything else, and I've got to do some of my duty by him, or I'll be the ruination of the child."

Tom did play hookey,
and he had a very good time.

Saturday morning was
come, and all the summer world
was brimming with life. Tom appeared
on the sidewalk with a bucket of whitewash and a long-handled brush. He surveyed
the fence, and a deep melancholy settled down
upon his spirit. Soon the free boys would come tripping along on all sorts of delicious expeditions, and
they would make a world of fun of him for having
to work, the very thought of it burned him like fire. At

this dark and hopeless moment an inspiration burst upon him! Nothing less than a great, magnificent inspiration.

He took up his brush and went tranquilly to work. Ben Rogers hove in sight presently, the very boy, of all boys, whose ridicule he had been dreading. Ben stared a moment and then said: "Hi, Yi! You're up a stump, ain't you!"

"Why, it's you, Ben! I warn't noticing."

"Say, I'm going in a-swimming, I am. Don't you wish you could? But of course you'd ruther work, wouldn't you? Course you would!"

Tom contemplated the boy a bit, and said:

"What do you call work?"

"Why, ain't that work?"

"Oh come, now, you don't mean to let on that you like it?"

The brush continued to move.

"Like it? Well, I don't see why I oughtn't to like it. Does a boy get a chance to whitewash a fence every day?"

That put the thing in a new light. Tom swept his brush daintily back and forth, Ben watching every move and getting more and more interested, more and more absorbed. Presently he said:

"Say, Tom, let me whitewash a little."

Tom considered, was about to consent; but he altered his mind:

"Ben, I'd like to, honest injun; but Aunt Polly, well, Jim wanted to do it, but she wouldn't let him; Sid wanted to do it, but she wouldn't let Sid. Now don't you see how I'm fixed? If you was to tackle this fence and anything was to happen to it . . ."

Sid is Tom's little brother who also lives with Aunt Polly. Jim is Aunt Polly's slave. Until 1865, it was legal for Americans to own slaves, who were almost always African Americans.

"Oh, shucks, I'll be just as careful. Now lemme try. Say, I'll give you the core of my apple. I'll give you all of it!"

Tom gave up the brush with reluctance in his face, but alacrity in his heart. By the time Ben was fagged out, Tom had traded the next chance to Billy Fisher for a kite, in good repair; and when he played out, Johnny Miller

bought in for a dead rat and a
string to swing it with, and so on,
and so on, hour after hour.
And when the middle of the
afternoon came,
from being a
poor poverty-
stricken boy
in the morn-
ing, Tom was

literally rolling in wealth. Tom presented himself before Aunt Polly. He said: "Mayn't I go and play now, aunt?"

"What, a'ready? How much have you done?"

"It's all done, aunt."

"Well, I never! There's no getting around it, you can work when you've a mind to, Tom. Well, go along and play; but mind you get back some time in a week, or I'll tan you."

As he was passing by the house where Jeff Thatcher lived, he saw a new girl in the garden; a lovely little

blue-eyed creature with yellow hair plaited into two long tails, white summer frock and embroidered pan-talettes. A certain Amy Lawrence vanished out of his heart and left not even a memory of herself behind.

He worshipped this new angel with furtive eye, till he saw that she had discovered him; then he pretended he did not know she was present, and began to "show off" in all sorts of absurd boyish ways, in order to win her admiration; but by and by, while he was in the midst of some dangerous gymnastic performances, he glanced aside and saw that the little girl was wending towards the house. Tom heaved a great sigh as she put her foot on the threshold. But his face lit up, right away, for she tossed a pansy over the fence a moment before she dis-appeared.

Chapter 2

HUCK AND THE DEAD CAT

As Tom wended to school he came upon the juvenile pariah of the village, Huckleberry Finn, son of the town drunkard. Huckleberry was cordially hated and dreaded by all the mothers of the town, because he was idle and lawless and vulgar and bad, and because all their children admired him so, and delighted in his forbidden society, and wished they dared to be like him. Tom was like the rest of the respectable boys, in that he envied Huckleberry his gaudy outcast condition, and was under strict orders not to play with him. So he

played with him every time he got a chance. Huckleberry was always dressed in the cast off clothes of full grown men, and they were in perennial bloom and fluttering with rags.

He slept on doorsteps in fine weather and in empty hogsheads in wet; he did not have to go to school or to church, or call any being master or obey anybody.

Tom hailed the romantic outcast:

"Hello, Huckleberry!"

"Hello yourself, and see how you like it."

"What's that you got?"

"Dead cat."

"Say, what is dead cats good for, Huck?"

"Good for? Cure warts with."

"Say, how do you cure 'em with dead cats?"

"Why, you take your cat and go and get in the grave-yard 'long about midnight where somebody that was wicked has been buried; and when it's midnight a devil will come, or maybe two or three, but you can't see 'em, you can only hear something like the wind, or maybe hear 'em talk; and when they're taking that feller away, you heave your cat after 'em and say, 'Devil follow corpse, cat follow devil, warts follow cat, I'm done with ye!' That'll fetch any wart."

"Say, Hucky, when you going to try the cat?"

"To-night. I reckon they'll come after old Hoss Williams to-night."

"Lemme go with you?"

"Of course, if you ain't afeard."

"Afeard! 'Tain't likely."

When Tom reached the little isolated frame school-house, he strode in briskly, with the manner of one who had come with all honest speed. He hung his hat on a peg and flung himself into his seat. The master was dozing, lulled by the frowsy hum of study. The interruption roused him.

"Thomas Sawyer!"

Tom knew that when his name was pronounced in full, it meant trouble.

"Sir!"

"Come up here. Now, sir, why are you late again, as usual?"

Tom was about to take refuge in a lie, when he saw

two long tails of yellow hair hanging down a back that he recognized by the electric sympathy of love; and by that form was the only vacant place on the girls' side of the school house. He instantly said:

"I stopped to talk with Huckleberry Finn."

"You, you did what?"

"Thomas Sawyer, this is the most astounding confession I have ever listened to. Take off your jacket."

The master's arm performed until it was tired and the stock of switches notably diminished. Then the order followed:

"Now, sir, go and sit with the girls! And let this be a warning to you."

He sat down upon the end of the pine bench and the girl hitched herself away from him with a toss of the head. Nudges and winks and whispers traversed the room, but Tom sat still.

In the 1800s, schools were usually made up of one large room for children in first grade all the way through high school. Boys and girls were usually separated with boys on one side of the room and girls on the other.

Presently the boy began to steal furtive glances at the girl. She observed it, "made a mouth" at him and gave him the back of her head for the space of a minute. When she cautiously faced around again, a peach lay before her. She thrust it away. Tom gently put it back.

She thrust it away again, but with less animosity. Tom patiently returned it to its place. Then she let it remain. Now the boy began to draw something on the slate, hiding his work with his left hand.

She begged to see. Tom said:

"Oh, it ain't anything."

"Yes it is. Now that you treat me so, I will see Tom." And she put her small hand on his and a little scuffle ensued, Tom pretending to resist in earnest but letting his hand slip by degrees till these words were revealed: "I LOVE YOU."

"Oh, you bad thing!" And she hit his hand a smart rap, but reddened and looked pleased, nevertheless.

Just at this juncture the boy felt a slow, fateful grip closing on his ear, and a steady lifting impulse. In that vice he was borne across the house and deposited in his own seat, under a peppering fire of giggles from the whole school. But although Tom's ear tingled, his heart was jubilant.

Chapter 3

A NIGHT IN THE GRAVEYARD

That night, he was dressed and out of the window and creeping along the roof of the "ell" on all fours. Huckleberry Finn was there, with his dead cat. The boys moved off and disappeared in the gloom. At the end of half an hour they were wading through the tall grass of the graveyard.

They found the sharp new heap they were seeking, and ensconced themselves within the protection of three great elms that grew in a bunch within a few feet of the grave.

Then they waited in silence for what
seemed a long time. Presently Tom seized
his comrade's arm and said:

"Sh!"

"What is it, Tom?" And
the two clung together with
beating hearts.

"Lord, Tom, they're coming!
They're coming, sure. What'll
we do?"

The boys bent their heads together and scarcely breathed. A muffled sound of voices floated up from the far end of the graveyard.

Some vague figures approached through the gloom. Presently Huckleberry whispered with a shudder:

"It's the devils sure enough. Three of 'em! Oh Lordy, Tom, we're goners! Can you pray?"

"I'll try, but don't you be afeard. I . . . "

"Sh!"

"What is it, Huck?"

"They're humans! One of 'em is, anyway. One of 'em's old Muff Potter's voice."

"Say, Huck, I know another o' them voices; it's Injun Joe."

"That so, that murderin' Indian! I'd druther they was devils a dern sight. What kin they be up to?"

"Here it is," said the third voice; and the owner of it held the lantern up and revealed the face of young Doctor Robinson.

Potter and Injun Joe were carrying a handbarrow with rope and a couple of shovels on it. They cast down their load and began to open the grave. They pried off the lid with their shovels, got out the body and dumped it rudely on the ground. The barrow was got ready and the corpse placed on it, covered with a blanket, and bound to its place with a rope. Potter took out a large spring knife and cut off the dangling end of the rope and then said:

Doc Robinson had hired Muff Potter and Injun Joe to dig up the grave so the doctor could use the body for medical research.

"Now the cussed thing's ready, Sawbones, and you'll just out with another five, or here she stays."

"That's the talk!" said Injun Joe.

"Look here, what does this mean?" said the doctor. "You required your pay in advance, and I've paid you."

"Yes, and you done more than that," said Injun Joe, approaching the doctor, who was now standing. "Five years ago you drove me away from your father's kitchen one night, when I come to ask for something to eat, and when I

swore I'd get even with you if it took a hundred years, your father had me jailed for a vagrant. Did you think I'd forget? The Injun blood ain't in me for nothing. And now I've got you, and you got to settle, you know!"

He was threatening the doctor, with his fist in his face, by this time. The doctor struck out suddenly and stretched the ruffian on the ground. Potter dropped his knife, and exclaimed:

"Here, now, don't you strike my pard!" and the next moment he had grappled with the doctor and the two were struggling with might and main, trampling the grass and tearing the ground with their heels. Injun Joe sprang to his feet, his eyes flaming with passion, snatched up Potter's knife, and went creeping, catlike and stooping, round and round about the combatants, seeking an opportunity. All at once the doctor flung himself free, seized the heavy headboard of Williams's grave and felled Potter to the earth with it, and in the same instant the Indian saw his chance and drove the knife to the hilt in the young man's breast. He reeled and fell partly upon Potter, flooding him with his blood, and the two frightened boys went speeding away in the dark.

The Indian muttered:

"That score is settled, damn you."

Then he robbed the body. After which he put the fatal knife in Potter's open right hand, and sat down on the dismantled coffin. Three, four, five minutes passed, and then Potter began to stir and moan. His hand closed upon the knife; he raised it, glanced at it, and let it fall, with a shudder. His eyes met Joe's.

"Lord, how is this, Joe?" he said.

"It's a dirty business," said Joe, without moving. "What did you do it for?"

"I! I never done it!"

"Look here! That kind of talk won't wash."

Potter trembled and grew white.

"I thought I'd got sober. I'd no business to drink to-night. I'm all in a muddle; can't recollect anything of it, hardly. Tell me, Joe, honest, now, old feller, did I do it? Tell me how it was, Joe. Oh, it's awful, and him so young and promising."

"Why, you two was scuffling, and he fetched you one with the headboard and you fell flat; and then up you come, all reeling and staggering like, and snatched the knife and jammed it into him, just as he fetched you another awful clip, and here are you laid dead as a wedge till now."

"Oh, I didn't know what I was doing. It was all on account of the whiskey and the excitement. You won't tell, will you, Joe?"

"No, no, you've always been fair and square with me, Muff Potter, and I won't go back on you. There, now, that's as fair as a man can say."

"Oh, Joe, you're an angel."

"Come, now, that's enough of that, this ain't any time for blubbering. You be off yonder way and I'll go this. Move, now, and don't leave any tracks behind you."

Chapter 4

THE BOYS BECOME PIRATES

The two boys flew on and on, towards the village, speechless with horror.

"Huckleberry, what do you reckon'll come of this?"

"If Doctor Robinson dies, I reckon hanging'll come of it."

Tom thought a while, then he said:

"Who'll tell? We?"

"What are you talking about? Suppose something happened and Injun Joe didn't hang? Why, he'd kill us some time or other."

"That's just what I was thinking to myself, Huck."

"Now, look-a-here, Tom, less take and swear to one another, that's what we got to do, swear to keep mum."

Close upon the hour of noon the whole village was suddenly electrified with the ghastly news.

A gory knife had been found close to the murdered man, and it had been recognized by somebody as belonging to Muff Potter, so the story ran.

All the town was drifting towards the graveyard. Tom's heartbreak vanished and he joined the procession. Arrived at the dreadful place, he wormed his small body through the crowd and saw the dismal spectacle.

Now Tom shivered from head to heel, for his eye fell upon the stolid face of Injun Joe. At this moment the crowd began to sway and struggle, and voices shouted, "It's him! It's him! He's coming himself."

"Who? Who?" from twenty voices.

"Muff Potter!"

"Hallo, he's stopped! Look out, he's turning! Don't let him get away!"

The crowd fell apart, now, and the Sheriff came through, ostentatiously leading Potter by the arm. The poor fellow's face was haggard, and his eyes showed the fear that was upon him. "I didn't do it, friends," he sobbed; "on my word and honor I never done it."

"Who's accused you?" shouted a voice.

This shot seemed to carry home. Potter lifted his face and looked around him with a pathetic hopelessness in his eyes. He saw Injun Joe, and exclaimed:

"Oh, Injun Joe, you promised me you'd never . . . "

"Is that your knife?" and it was thrust before him by the Sheriff.

Potter would have fallen if they had not caught him and eased him to the ground. Then he said:

"Tell 'em, Joe, tell 'em, it ain't no use any more."

Then Huckleberry and Tom stood dumb and staring, and heard the stony-hearted liar reel off his serene statement. Tom's fearful secret and gnawing conscience disturbed his sleep for as much as a week after this.

Tom's mind was made up now. He was gloomy and desperate. He was a forsaken, friendless boy, he said; nobody loved him; when they found out what they had driven him to, perhaps they would be sorry. Yes, they had forced him to it at last: he would lead a life of crime. Then the sobs came thick and fast.

Just at this point he met his soul's sworn comrade, Joe Harper. As the two boys walked sorrowing along, they made a new compact to stand by each other and be brothers and never separate till death relieved them of their troubles. Then they began to lay their plans. Joe was for being a hermit, but after listening to Tom, he conceded that there were some conspicuous advantages about a life of crime, and so he consented to be a pirate.

Three miles below St. Petersburg, at a point where the Mississippi River was a trifle over a mile wide, there was a long, narrow, wooded island, with a shallow bar at the head of it, and this offered well as a rendezvous. It was not inhabited. So Jackson's Island was chosen. Then they hunted up Huckleberry Finn, and he joined them promptly. They presently separated to meet at a lonely spot on the river bank two miles above the village at the favorite hour, which was midnight. There was a small log raft there which they meant to capture. Each would bring hooks and lines, and such provisions as he could steal in the most dark and mysterious way, as became outlaws.

The town of St. Petersburg in *The Adventures of Tom Sawyer* is based on Mark Twain's home town of Hannibal, Missouri. Many of the characters in St. Petersburg are based on people Mark Twain grew up with in Hannibal.

About midnight Tom arrived with a boiled ham and a few trifles, and stopped in a dense undergrowth on a small bluff overlooking the meeting-place. Then a guarded voice said:

"Who goes there?"

"Tom Sawyer, the Black Avenger of the Spanish Main. Name your names."

"Huck Finn the Red-Handed, and Joe Harper the Terror of the Seas." Tom had furnished these titles, from his favorite literature.

Tom's "favorite literature" includes what are called "dime novels." These were inexpensive books that became very popular in the mid-1800s and were full of stories of action and adventure.

"'Tis well. Give the countersign."

Two hoarse whispers delivered the same awful word simultaneously to the brooding night:

"Blood!"

They shoved off, presently, Tom in command, Huck at the left oar and Joe at the forward. The raft drew beyond the middle of the river; the boys pointed her head right, and then lay on their oars. The river was not high, so there was not more than a two or three mile current. About two in the morning the raft grounded on the bar two hundred yards above the head of the island, and they waded back and forth until they had landed their freight. They built a fire against the side of a great log twenty or thirty steps within the somber depths of the forest, and then cooked some bacon in the frying pan for supper.

"Ain't it jolly?" said Joe.

"It's nuts!" said Tom. "What would the boys say if they could see us?"

"Say? Well, they'd just die to be here, hey, Hucky!"

"I reckon so," said Huckleberry; "It's just the life for me," said Tom. "You don't have to get up, mornings, you don't have to go to school, and wash, and all that blame foolishness."

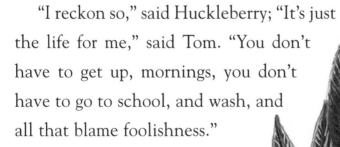

Presently Huck said:

"What do pirates have to do?"

Tom said: "Oh, they have just a bully time, take ships and burn them, and get the money and bury it in awful places in their island where there's ghosts and things to watch it."

Gradually their talk died out and drowsiness began to steal upon the eyelids of the little waifs.

⟨ Chapter 5 ⟩

THE BOYS DISCOVER THEY HAVE DROWNED

When Tom awoke in the morning, he wondered where he was. He sat up and rubbed his eyes and looked around. Then he comprehended.

Tom stirred up the other pirates and they all clattered away with a shout, and in a minute or two were stripped and chasing after and tumbling over each other in the shallow limpid water of the white sandbar. A vagrant current or a slight rise in the river had carried off their raft, but this only gratified them, since its going was something like burning

the bridge between them
and civilization.

They came back to camp
wonderfully refreshed, glad-
hearted, and ravenous; and they soon had the
camp fire blazing up again. While Joe was slicing
bacon for breakfast, Tom and Huck asked him

to hold on a minute. They stepped to a promising nook in the river bank and threw in their lines; almost immediately they had reward. They fried the fish with the bacon, and were astonished; for no fish had ever seemed so delicious before.

They lay around in the shade, after breakfast, and then went off through the woods on an exploring expedition. They took a swim about every hour, so it was close upon the middle of the afternoon when they got

back to camp. For some time, now, the boys had been dully conscious of a peculiar sound in the distance, but now this mysterious sound became more pronounced. There was a long silence, then a deep, sullen boom came floating down out of the distance.

"What is it!" exclaimed Joe, under his breath.

"I wonder," said Tom in a whisper.

They waited a time that seemed an age, and then the same muffled boom troubled the solemn hush.

"Let's go and see."

They sprang to their feet and hurried to the shore towards the town. They parted the bushes on the bank and peered out over the water. The little steam ferryboat was about a mile below the village, drifting with the current. Her broad deck seemed crowded with people. Presently a great jet of white smoke burst from the ferryboat's side, and as it expanded and rose in a lazy cloud, that same dull throb of sound was borne to the listeners again.

"I know now!" exclaimed Tom; "somebody's drownded!"

"By jings, I wish I was over there, now," said Joe.

"I do too," said Huck, "I'd give heaps to know who it is."

Presently a revealing thought flashed through Tom's mind, and he exclaimed:

"Boys, I know who's drownded, it's us!"

They felt like heroes in an instant. Here was a gorgeous triumph; they were missed, they were mourned, hearts were breaking on their account; tears were being shed, and best of all, the departed were the talk of the whole town. This was fine. It was worthwhile to be a pirate, after all.

As twilight drew on, the pirates returned to camp. But when the shadows of night closed them in, the excitement was gone, and Tom and Joe could not keep back thoughts of certain persons at home who were not enjoying this fine frolic as much as they were.

As the night deepened, Huck began to nod, and presently to snore. Joe followed next. Tom lay upon his elbow motionless, watching the two intently. At last he got up cautiously, on his knees, and went searching among the grass and the flickering reflections flung by the camp fire. He picked up and inspected several large semi-cylinders of the thin white bark of a sycamore, and finally chose two which seemed to suit him. Then he knelt by the fire and painfully wrote something upon each of these with his "red keel"; one he rolled up and put in his jacket pocket, and the other he put in Joe's hat and removed it to a little distance from the owner. Then he tiptoed his way cautiously among the trees till he felt that he was out of hearing, and straightway broke into a keen run in the direction of the sandbar.

Tom also put into the hat certain schoolboy treasures of almost inestimable value—among them a lump of chalk, an India-rubber ball, three fishhooks, and one of that kind of marbles known as a "sure-'nough crystal."

Chapter 6

TOM RETURNS HOME MOMENTARILY

Shortly before ten o'clock he came out into an open place opposite the village, and saw the ferryboat lying in the shadow of the trees and the high bank. Everything was quiet under the blinking stars. He crept down the bank, slipped into the water, swam three or four strokes and climbed into the skiff that did "yawl" duty at the boat's stern. He laid himself down under the thwarts and waited.

Presently the cracked bell tapped and a voice gave the order to "cast off." At the end of a long twelve or

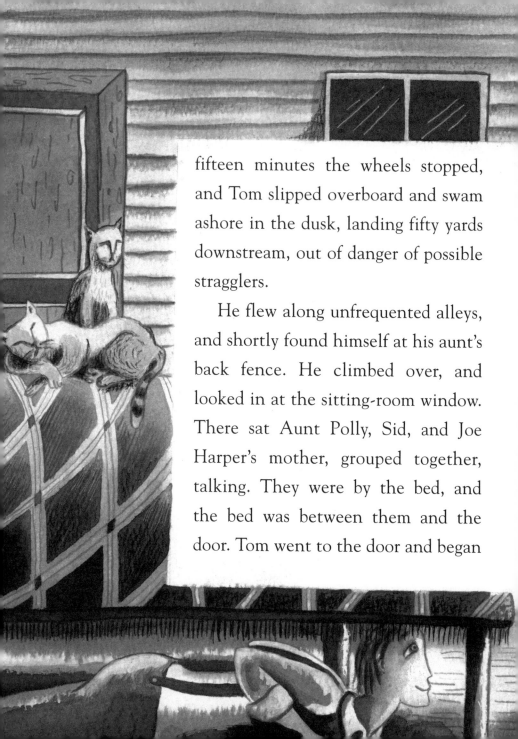

fifteen minutes the wheels stopped, and Tom slipped overboard and swam ashore in the dusk, landing fifty yards downstream, out of danger of possible stragglers.

He flew along unfrequented alleys, and shortly found himself at his aunt's back fence. He climbed over, and looked in at the sitting-room window. There sat Aunt Polly, Sid, and Joe Harper's mother, grouped together, talking. They were by the bed, and the bed was between them and the door. Tom went to the door and began

to softly lift the latch; then he
pressed gently and the door yielded
a crack; "What makes the candle blow so?" said Aunt
Polly. "Why, that door's open, I believe."

Tom disappeared under the bed just in time.

"But as I was saying,"
said Aunt Polly, "he never
meant any harm, and he
was the best-hearted boy
that ever was," and
she began to cry.

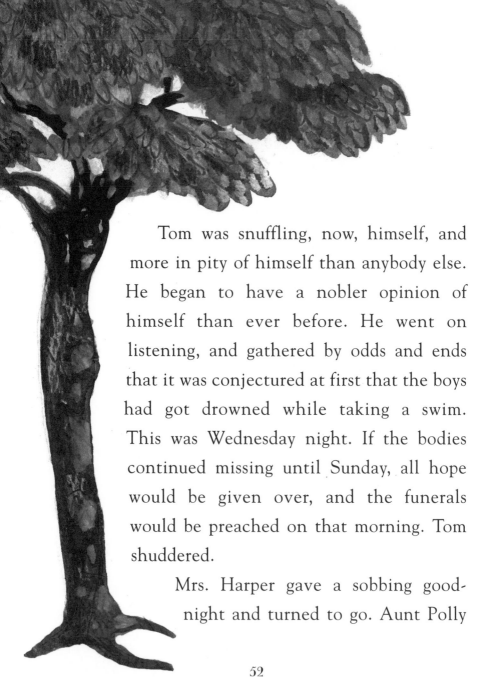

Tom was snuffling, now, himself, and more in pity of himself than anybody else. He began to have a nobler opinion of himself than ever before. He went on listening, and gathered by odds and ends that it was conjectured at first that the boys had got drowned while taking a swim. This was Wednesday night. If the bodies continued missing until Sunday, all hope would be given over, and the funerals would be preached on that morning. Tom shuddered.

Mrs. Harper gave a sobbing good-night and turned to go. Aunt Polly knelt down and prayed for Tom so touchingly, so appealingly, that he was weltering in tears again, long before she was through.

He had to keep still long after she went to bed, for she kept making broken-hearted ejaculations from time to time, tossing unrestfully, and turning over. But at last she was still. Now the boy stole out, rose gradually by the bedside, and stood regarding her. His heart was full of pity for her. He took out his sycamore scroll and placed it by the candle. But something occurred to him. His face lighted with a happy solution of his thought; he put the bark hastily in his pocket. Then he bent over and kissed the faded lips, and straightway made his stealthy exit.

It was broad daylight before he paused, dripping, upon the threshold of the camp, and heard Joe say:

"No, Tom's true blue, Huck, and he'll come back. He won't desert. He knows that would be a disgrace to a

pirate, and Tom's too proud for that sort of thing. He's up to something or other. Now I wonder what?"

"Well, the things is ours, anyway, ain't they?"

"Pretty near, but not yet, Huck. The writing says they are if he ain't back to breakfast."

"Which he is!" exclaimed Tom, with fine dramatic effect, stepping grandly into camp. "I want to tell you something!"

When he got to where they were, he began unfolding his secret, and they listened moodily till at last they saw the "point" he was driving at, and then they set up a war whoop of applause and said it was "splendid!" The lads went at their sports again with a will, chatting all the time about Tom's stupendous plan and admiring the genius of it.

Chapter 7

THE FUNERAL

But there was no hilarity in the little town that same tranquil Saturday afternoon. The Harpers, and Aunt Polly's family, were being put into mourning, with great grief and many tears. An unusual quiet possessed the village.

Becky Thatcher found herself moping about the deserted schoolhouse yard, and feeling very melancholy. But she found nothing there to comfort her.

When the Sunday-school hour was finished, the next morning, the bell began to toll, instead of ringing in the usual way. The villagers began to gather, loitering a moment in the vestibule to converse in whispers about

the sad event. None could remember when the little church had been so full before. There was finally a waiting pause, and then Aunt Polly entered, followed by the Harper family, all in deep black, and the whole congregation, the old minister as well, rose reverently and stood until the mourners were seated in the front pew. And then the minister spread his hands abroad and prayed. The congregation became more and more moved, till at last the whole company broke down and joined the weeping mourners in a chorus of anguished sobs, the preacher himself giving way to his feelings, and crying in the pulpit.

A moment later the church door creaked; the minister raised his streaming eyes above his handkerchief, and stood transfixed! First one and then another pair of eyes followed the minister's, and then almost with one impulse the congregation rose and stared while the three dead boys came marching up the aisle, Tom in the lead, Joe next, and Huck, a ruin of drooping rags, sneaking sheepishly in the rear! They had been hid in the unused gallery listening to their own funeral sermon!

Suddenly the minister shouted at the top of his voice: "Praise God from whom all blessings flow. Sing, and put your hearts in it!"

And they did. Tom Sawyer the Pirate looked around upon the envying juveniles about him and confessed in his heart that this was the proudest moment in his life.

That was Tom's great secret, the scheme to return home with his brother pirates and attend their own funerals. They had paddled over to the Missouri shore on a log, at dusk on Saturday, slept in the woods, and crept into the gallery of the church.

What a hero Tom was become, now! He did not go skipping and prancing, but moved with a dignified swagger as became a pirate who felt that the public eye was on him. Tom decided that he could be independent of Becky Thatcher now. Glory was sufficient. Now that he was distinguished, maybe she would be wanting to "make up." Well, let her. Presently she arrived. Tom pretended not to see her. He moved away and joined a group of boys and girls and began to talk. Soon he observed that she was tripping gaily back and forth with flushed face and dancing eyes, and that she seemed to cast a conscious eye in his direction at such times, too.

Becky was upset with Tom after she found out that Tom used to be in love with Amy Lawrence.

At recess Tom kept drifting about to find Becky and lacerate her with the performance. At last he spied her, but there was a sudden falling of his mercury. She was sitting cozily on a little bench behind the schoolhouse looking at a picture-book with Alfred Temple. Jealousy ran red-hot through Tom's veins.

"Any other boy!" Tom thought, grating his teeth. "Any boy in the whole town but that Saint Louis smarty."

Chapter 8

TOM CONFESSES TO AUNT POLLY

om arrived in a dreary mood, and the first thing his aunt said to him showed him that he had brought his sorrows to an unpromising market:

"Tom, I've a notion to skin you alive!"

"Auntie, what have I done?"

"Well, you've done enough. Here I go over to Sereny Harper, when lo and behold she'd found out from Joe that you was over here and heard all the talk we had one night."

"Auntie, I wish I hadn't done it, it was to tell you

not to be uneasy about us, because we hadn't got drownded. An' when you got to talking about the funeral, I just got all full of the idea of our coming and hiding in the church, and I couldn't somehow bear to spoil it. So I just put the bark back in my pocket and kept mum."

"What bark?"

"The bark I had wrote on to tell you we'd gone pirating. I wish, now, you'd waked up when I kissed you, I do, honest."

"Did you kiss me, Tom?"

"Why, yes, I did."

"What did you kiss me for, Tom?"

"Because I loved you so, and I was so sorry."

The words sounded like truth. The old lady could not hide a tremor in her voice when she said:

"Kiss me again, Tom! And be off with you to school."

There was something about Aunt Polly's manner, when she kissed Tom, that made him light hearted and happy again. He started to school and had the luck of coming upon Becky Thatcher at the head of Meadow Lane. "I acted mighty mean today, Becky, and I'm so sorry. I won't ever, ever do it that way again, as long as ever I live. Please make up, won't you?"

"I'll thank you to keep yourself to

yourself, Mr. Thomas Sawyer. I'll never speak to you again."

She tossed her head and passed on. Poor girl, she did not know how fast she was nearing trouble herself. The master, Mr. Dobbins, had reached middle age with an unsatisfied ambition. The darling of his desires was to be a doctor, but poverty had decreed that he should be nothing higher than a village schoolmaster. Every day he took a mysterious book out of his desk and absorbed himself in it at times when no classes were reciting. He kept that book under lock and key. Now, as Becky was passing by the desk, which stood near the door, she noticed that the key was in the lock! She glanced around; found herself alone, and the next instant she had the book in her hands. The title page, Professor Somebody's ANATOMY, carried no information to her mind; so she began to turn the leaves. At that moment a shadow fell on the page and Tom Sawyer stepped in at the door. Becky snatched at the book to close it, and had the hard luck to tear the pictured page half down the middle. She thrust the volume into the desk, turned the key, and burst out crying with shame and vexation.

Anatomy is the structure of an animal or plant. For example, your skeleton is a part of your anatomy.

"Tom Sawyer, you are just as mean as you can be, to sneak up on a person and look at what they're looking at. You know you're going to tell on me, oh no, what shall I do! I'll be whipped, and I never was whipped in school."

And she flung out of the house with a new explosion of crying.

Chapter 9

MUFF POTTER'S TRIAL

whole hour drifted by. By and by, Mr. Dobbins took out his book and settled himself in his chair to read! Tom shot a glance at Becky. There was silence while one might count ten, the master was gathering his wrath. Then he spoke:

"Who tore this book?"

There was not a sound. A thought shot like lightning through Tom's brain. He sprang to his feet and shouted, "I done it!"

The surprise, the gratitude, the adoration that shone upon him out of poor Becky's eyes seemed pay enough for a hundred floggings.

Inspired by the splendor of his own act, he took without an outcry the most merciless flogging that even Mr. Dobbins had ever administered. Tom went to bed that night planning vengeance against Alfred Temple; but even the longing for vengeance had to give way, soon, to pleasanter musing, and he fell asleep at last with Becky's latest words lingering dreamily in his ear,

"Tom, how could you be so noble!"

The murder trial came on in the court. It became the absorbing topic of village talk immediately. Tom could not get away from it. Every reference to the murder sent a shudder to his heart. At the end of the second day the village talk was to the effect that Injun Joe's evidence stood firm and unshaken, and that there was not the slightest question as to what the jury's verdict would be. All the village flocked to the court-house the next morning, for this was to be the great day. After a long wait the jury filed in and took their places; shortly afterwards, Potter, pale and haggard, timid and hopeless, was brought in, with chains upon him, and seated where all the curious eyes could stare at him. Counsel for the defense rose and said:

"Your honor, in our remarks at the opening of this trial, we foreshadowed our purpose to prove that our client did this fearful deed while under the influence of a blind and irresponsible delirium produced by drink. We have changed our mind. We shall not offer that plea. Call Thomas Sawyer!"

"Thomas Sawyer, where were you on the seventeenth of June, about the hour of midnight?"

Tom glanced at Injun Joe's face and his tongue failed him. After a few moments, however, the boy got a little of his strength back, "In the graveyard!"

"Were you anywhere near Horse Williams's grave?"

"Yes, sir."

"Now, my boy, tell us everything that occurred, tell it in your own way, don't skip anything, and don't be afraid."

Tom began, hesitatingly at first, but as he warmed to his subject his words flowed more and more easily;

every eye fixed itself upon him. The strain upon pent emotion reached its climax when the boy said:

"And as the doctor fetched the board around and Muff Potter fell, Injun Joe jumped with the knife and . . ."

Crash! Quick as lightning the Indian sprang for a window, tore his way through all opposers, and was gone!

Tom was a glittering hero once more, the pet of the old, the envy of the young. Tom's days were days of splendor and exultation to him, but his nights were seasons of horror. Injun Joe infested all his dreams, and always with doom in his eye. He felt sure he could never draw a safe breath again until that man was dead and he had seen the corpse.

Rewards had been offered, the country had been scoured, but no Injun Joe was found. The slow days drifted on, and each left behind it a slightly lightened weight of apprehension.

⟨ Chapter 10 ⟩

TREASURE IN THE HAUNTED HOUSE

There comes a time in every rightly-constructed boy's life when he has a raging desire to go somewhere and dig for hidden treasure. This desire suddenly came upon Tom one day. Presently he stumbled upon Huck Finn the Red-handed. Huck was willing.

"Where'll we dig?" said Huck.

"Oh, most anywhere."

"Why, is it hid all around?"

"No, indeed it ain't. It's hid in mighty particular places, Huck."

"Who hides it?"

"Why, robbers, of course, who'd you reckon?"

"They always bury it under a ha'nted house or on an island, or under a dead tree that's got one limb sticking out. Well, we've tried Jackson's Island a little, and we can try it again some time; and there's the old ha'nted house up

the Still-House branch, and there's lots of dead-limb trees. What'll it be?"

"The ha'nted house. That's it!"

When they reached the haunted house they were afraid, for a moment, to venture in.

In a little while familiarity modified their fears and they gave the place a critical and interested examination. Next they wanted to look upstairs. They threw their tools into

a corner and made the ascent. They were about to go down and begin work again when,

"Sh!" said Tom.

"What is it?" whispered Huck.

"Sh! . . . There! . . . Hear it?"

"Yes! . . . Oh, my! Let's run!"

"Keep still! Don't you budge! They're coming right towards the door."

The boys stretched themselves upon the floor with their eyes to knot-holes in the planking, and lay waiting, in a misery of fear. Two men entered.

"No, I've thought it all over, and I don't like it. It's dangerous."

"Dangerous! Milksop!"

This voice made the boys gasp and quake. It was Injun Joe's! There was silence for some time. Then Joe said:

"Look here, lad, you go back up the river where you belong. Wait there till you hear from me. I'll take the chances on dropping into this town just once more, for a look. We'll do that 'dangerous' job after I've spied around a little and think things look well for it. Then for Texas! We'll leg it together!"

Both men presently fell to yawning, and Injun Joe said:

"Nearly time for us to be moving, pard. What'll we do with what little swag we've got left?"

"I don't know, leave it here as we've always done, I reckon. No use to take it away till we start south. Six hundred and fifty in silver's something to carry."

"Yes, but look here; it may be a good while before I get the right chance at that job; we'll just regularly bury it, and bury it deep."

"Good idea," said the comrade, who walked across the room, knelt down, raised one of the rearward hearthstones and took out a bag that jingled pleasantly.

He subtracted from it twenty or thirty dollars for himself and as much for Injun Joe, and passed the bag to the latter, who was on his knees in the corner, now, digging with his bowie knife.

The boys forgot all their fears, all their miseries in an instant. With gloating eyes they watched every movement. Joe's knife struck upon something.

"Hello!" said he.

"What is it?" said his comrade.

"Half rotten plank, no, it's a box, I believe."

"Man, it's money!"

"Pard, there's thousands of dollars here," said Injun Joe.

"'Twas always said that Murrel's gang used around here one summer," the stranger observed.

Murrel's gang was a legendary group of robbers and counterfeiters who terrorized the towns along the banks of the Mississippi River.

"I know it," said Injun Joe; "and this looks like it, I should say."

"Now you won't need to do that job."

The Indian frowned.

"You don't know me. Least you don't know all about that thing. 'Tain't robbery altogether, it's revenge!" and a wicked light flamed in his eye.

"Well, if you say so; what'll we do with this, bury it again?"

"We'll take it to my den."

"You mean No. 1?"

"No, No. 2, under the cross. The other place is bad, too common."

"All right. It's nearly dark enough to start."

Shortly afterwards they slipped out of the house in the deepening twilight, and moved towards the river with their precious box.

Tom and Huck rose up, weak but vastly relieved, and stared after them through the chinks between the logs

of the house. Then a ghastly
thought occurred to Tom.

"Revenge? What if he
means *us*, Huck!"

"Oh, don't!" said
Huck, nearly fainting.

"No. 2, What do you
reckon it is?"

"I do'no. It's too
deep. Say, Huck, maybe
it's the number of a
house!"

"Goody! . . . No, Tom, that ain't it. If it is, it ain't in this one horse town. They ain't no numbers here."

"Well, that's so. Lemme think a minute. Here, it's the number of a room in a tavern, you know!"

"Oh, that's the trick! They ain't only two taverns. We can find out quick."

"You stay here, Huck, till I come."

He was gone half an hour. He found that in the best tavern, No. 2 had long been occupied by a young lawyer. In the less ostentatious house, No. 2 was a mystery. The tavern keeper's young son said it was kept locked all the time, and he never saw anybody go into it or come out of it except at night and that there was a light in there the night before.

"Huck. I reckon that's the very No. 2 we're after."

"Now, if we watch every night, we'll be dead sure to see Injun Joe go out, some time or other, then we'll snatch that box quicker'n lightning."

"Well, I'm agreed. I'll watch the whole night long, and I'll do it every night, too, if you'll do the other part of the job."

"Agreed!"

Chapter 11

A PICNIC AND A TRIP TO THE CAVE

The first thing Tom heard on Friday morning was a glad piece of news. Becky teased her mother to appoint the next day for a long promised and long delayed picnic, and she consented. The invitations were sent out before sunset, and straightway the young folks of the village were thrown into a fever of preparation and pleasurable anticipation.

Morning came, eventually, and by ten or eleven o'clock a giddy and rollicking company were gathered at Judge Thatcher's, and everything was ready for a start. The old ferryboat was chartered for the occasion; presently the gay throng filed up the main street laden with provision baskets. The last thing Mrs. Thatcher said to Becky, was:

"You'll not get back till late. Perhaps you'd better stay all night with some of the girls that live near the ferry landing, child."

"Then I'll stay with Suzy Harper, mamma."

"Very well. And mind and behave yourself and don't be any trouble."

The parents did not go with the children on the picnic. The children were considered safe enough under the wings of a few young ladies of eighteen and a few young gentlemen of twenty-three or thereabouts.

Three miles below town the ferryboat stopped at the mouth of a woody hollow and tied up. The crowd swarmed ashore and soon the forest distances and craggy heights echoed far and near with shoutings and laughter. After the feast somebody shouted:

"Who's ready for the cave?"

Everybody was. Bundles of candles were produced, and straightway there was a general scamper up the hill. The mouth of the cave was high up the hillside, an opening shaped like the letter A. Its massive oaken door stood unbarred. It was said that one might wander days and nights together through its intricate tangle of rifts and chasms, and never find the end of the cave. No

man "knew" the cave. That was an impossible thing. Most of the young men knew a portion of it, and it was not customary to venture much beyond this known portion. Tom Sawyer knew as much of the cave as anyone.

The cave contained different areas with various names, such as "The Drawing Room," "The Cathedral," and "Aladdin's Palace."

By and by, one group after another came straggling back to the mouth of the cave. Then they were astonished to find that they had been taking no note of time and that night was about at hand. However, this sort of close to the day's adventures was romantic and therefore satisfactory. When the ferryboat with her wild freight pushed into the stream, nobody cared sixpence for the wasted time but the captain of the craft.

Huck was already upon his watch when the ferryboat's lights went glinting past the wharf. Ten o'clock came, eleven o'clock came, and the tavern lights were put out; darkness everywhere, now.

A noise fell upon his ear. The next moment two men brushed by him, and one seemed to have something under his arm. It must be that box! So they were going to remove the treasure. Why call Tom now? It would be absurd, the men would get away with the box and never be found again. No, he would stick to

their wake and follow
them. They moved up the
river street three blocks,
then turned to the left up a
cross street. They passed
by the old Welshman's
house, half-way up the
hill, without hes-
itating, and still
climbed upward.

They passed on, up the summit. They plunged into the narrow path between the tall sumach bushes, and were at once hidden in the gloom. He knew he was within five steps of the stile leading into Widow Douglas's grounds.

The Widow Douglas was fair, smart, and forty, a generous good-hearted soul and well-to-do, her hill mansion the only palace in town.

Now there was a low voice, a very low voice, Injun Joe's.

"Damn her, maybe she's got company, there's lights, late as it is."

"Yes. Well, there is company there, I reckon. Better give it up."

"Give it up, and I was just leaving this country forever! I don't care for her swag, you may have it. But her husband was rough on me, and mainly he was the justice of the peace that jugged me for a vagrant. And that ain't all. He had me horsewhipped! He took advantage of me and died. But I'll take it out on her."

"Well, if it's got to be done, let's get at it, and the quicker the better, I'm all in a shiver."

"Do it now? And company there? No, we'll wait till the lights are out, there's no hurry."

TRACK 12

Chapter 12

HUCKLEBERRY FINN SAVES WIDOW DOUGLAS

*H*uck flew. Down, down he sped, till he reached the Welshman's. He banged at the door, and presently the heads of the old man and his two stalwart sons were thrust from windows.

"What's the row there? Who's banging? What do you want?"

"Huckleberry Finn, quick, let me in!"

"Huckleberry Finn, indeed! It ain't a name to open many doors, I judge! But let him in, lads, and let's see what's the trouble."

"Please don't ever tell I told you," were Huck's first words when he got in. "Please don't, I'd be killed, sure, but the widow's been good friends to me sometimes, and I want to tell, I will tell if you'll promise you won't ever say it was me."

Three minutes later the old man and his sons, well

armed, were up on the hill, and just entering the sumach path on tiptoe, their weapons in their hands. There was a lagging, anxious silence, and then all of a sudden there was an explosion of firearms and a cry. Huck waited for no particulars. He sprang away and sped down the hill as fast as his legs could carry him.

Although the Widow Douglas wanted to know who helped save her, the Welshman kept his promise and never told it was Huck who discovered Injun Joe.

As the earliest suspicion of dawn appeared on Sunday morning, Huck came groping up the hill and rapped gently at the Welshman's door.

"Do please let me in! It's only Huck Finn!"

The door was quickly unlocked, and he entered.

"I was awful scared," said Huck, "and I run. I took out

when the pis-
tols went off,
and I didn't stop
for three mile. And
I come before day-
light becuz I didn't
want to run across
them devils, even if
they was dead."

"No, they ain't dead,
lad, we are sorry enough
for that. You see we knew
right where to put our
hands on them, by
your description.
But they were off in

a jiffy, those villains. As soon as we lost the sound of their feet we quit chasing, and went down and stirred up the constables. They got a posse together, and went off to guard the river bank, and as soon as it is light the sheriff and a gang are going to beat up the woods."

There was no Sabbath school during day-school vacation, but everybody was early at church. When the sermon was finished, Judge Thatcher's wife dropped alongside of Mrs. Harper as she moved down the aisle with the crowd and said:

"Is my Becky going to sleep all day? I just expected she would be tired to death."

"Your Becky?"

"Yes," with a startled look, "didn't she stay with you last night?"

"Why, no."

Mrs. Thatcher turned pale, and sank into a pew, just as Aunt Polly, talking briskly with a friend, passed by. Aunt Polly said:

"Good morning, Mrs. Thatcher. Good morning, Mrs. Harper. I've got a boy that's turned up missing. I reckon my Tom stayed at your house last night, one of you. And now he's afraid to come to church. I've got to settle with him."

Mrs. Thatcher shook her head feebly and turned paler than ever.

"He didn't stay with us," said Mrs. Harper, beginning to look uneasy. Children were anxiously questioned, and young teachers. They all said they had not noticed whether Tom and Becky were on board the ferryboat on the homeward trip. One young man finally blurted out his fear that they were still in the cave! The alarm swept from lip to lip, from group to group, from street to street, and within five minutes the bells were wildly clanging and the whole town was up. Before the horror was half an hour old, two hundred men were pouring down high-road and river towards the cave.

Three dreadful days and nights dragged their tedious hours along, and the village sank into a hopeless stupor. No one had heart for anything.

Chapter 13

TOM AND BECKY LOST IN THE CAVE

Now to return to Tom and Becky's share in the picnic. They tripped along the murky aisles with the rest of the company, still drifting along and talking, they scarcely noticed that they were now in a part of the cave whose walls were not frescoed. Presently they came to a place where a little stream of water, trickling over a ledge and carrying a limestone sediment with it, had, in the slow-dragging ages, formed a laced and ruffled Niagara in gleaming and imperishable stone. Tom squeezed his small body behind it in order to illuminate

it for Becky's gratification. He found that it curtained a sort of steep natural stairway, which was enclosed between narrow walls, and at once the ambition to be a discoverer seized him. Becky responded to his call, and they made a smoke mark for future guidance and started upon their quest. They wound this way and that, far down into the secret depths of the cave, made another mark and branched off in search of novelties to tell the upper world about. Becky said:

"Why, I didn't notice, but it seems ever so long since I heard any of the others."

"Come to think, Becky, we are away down below them, and I don't know how far away north, or south, or east, or whichever it is. We couldn't hear them here."

Becky grew apprehensive.

"I wonder how long we've been down here, Tom. We better start back."

"Yes, I reckon we better. Perhaps we better."

It was but a little while before a certain indecision in his manner revealed another fearful fact to Becky, he could not find his way back!

By and by, fatigue began to assert its claims; the children tried to pay no attention, but at last Becky's frail limbs refused to carry her farther. She sat down.

Mark Twain Cave in Hannibal, Missouri, is said to have been a hideout for the infamous Jesse James as well as slaves who were searching for freedom via the Underground Railroad.

A long time after this, they could not tell how long, Tom said they must go softly and listen for dripping water, they must find a spring. They found one presently, and Tom said it was time to rest again. Both were cruelly tired, yet Becky said she thought she could go a little farther. She was surprised to hear Tom dissent. She could not understand it. Tom was silent a moment. Then he said:

"Becky, can you bear it if I tell you something?"

Becky's face paled, but she said she thought she could.

"Well, then, Becky, we must stay here, where there's water to drink. That little piece is our last candle!"

Becky gave loose to tears and wailings. Tom did what he could to comfort her, but with little effect.

The weary time dragged on; they slept again, and awoke famished and woe-stricken. Tom believed it must be Tuesday by this time.

Now an idea struck him. There were some side passages near at hand. He took a kite-line from his pocket, tied it to a projection, and he and Becky started, Tom in the lead, unwinding the line as he groped along. At the end of twenty steps the corridor ended in a "jumping-off place." Tom got down on his knees and felt below, and then as far around the corner as he could reach with his hands conveniently; and at the moment, not twenty yards away, a human hand, holding a candle, appeared from behind a rock! Tom lifted up a glorious shout, and instantly that hand was followed by the body it belonged to, Injun Joe's! Tom was paralyzed; he could not move. He was careful to keep from Becky what it was he had seen. He told her he had only shouted "for luck."

But hunger and wretchedness rise superior to fears in the long run. Another tedious wait at the spring and another long sleep brought changes. Becky was very weak. She told Tom to go with the kite-line and explore if he chose; but she implored him to come back every little while and speak to her. Tom made a show of being

confident of finding
the searchers or an escape from
the cave; then he took the kite-
line in his hand and went groping
down one of the passages on his hands
and knees, distressed with hunger and
sick with bodings of coming doom.

Chapter 14

TOM AND BECKY ARE FOUND

Tuesday afternoon came, and waned to the twilight. The village of St. Petersburg still mourned.

Away in the middle of the night a wild peal burst from the village bells, and in a moment the streets were swarming with frantic half-clad people, who shouted, "Turn out! Turn out! They're found! They're found!"

The village was illuminated; nobody went to bed again; it was the greatest night the little town had ever seen. During the first half hour a procession of

villagers filed through Judge Thatcher's house, seized the saved ones and kissed them, squeezed Mrs. Thatcher's hand, tried to speak but couldn't, and drifted out raining tears all over the place.

Aunt Polly's happiness was complete, and Mrs. Thatcher's nearly so. Tom lay upon a sofa and told the history of the wonderful adventure, and closed with a description of how he left Becky and went on an exploring expedition; how he followed two avenues as far as his kite-line would reach; how he followed a third to the fullest stretch of the kite-line, and was about to turn back when he glimpsed a far off speck that looked like daylight; dropped the line and groped towards it, pushed his head and shoulders through a small hole, and saw the broad Mississippi rolling by! He described how he labored with her and convinced her; and how she almost died for joy when she had groped to where she actually saw the blue speck of daylight; how he pushed his way out of the hole and then helped her out; how they sat there and cried for gladness; how some men came along in a skiff and Tom hailed them and told them their situation and their famished condition; how the men took them aboard, rowed to a house, gave them supper, made them rest till two or three hours after dark and then brought them home.

Mammoth Cave National Park in Kentucky is the world's longest cave system. More than 365 miles have been explored so far.

About a fortnight after Tom's rescue from the cave, he started off to visit Huck. Judge Thatcher's house was on Tom's way, and he stopped to see Becky. The Judge and some friends set Tom to talking, and someone asked him ironically if he wouldn't like to go to the cave again. Tom said yes he thought he wouldn't mind it. The Judge said:

"Well, there are others just like you, Tom, I've not the least doubt. But we have taken care of that. Nobody will get lost in that cave any more."

"Why?"

"Because I had its big door sheathed with boiler iron two weeks ago, and triple locked, and I've got the keys."

Tom turned as white as a sheet.

"What's the matter, boy?"

"Oh, Judge, Injun Joe's in the cave!"

Chapter 15

TOM AND HUCK BECOME RICH

When the cave door was unlocked, Injun Joe lay stretched upon the ground, dead, with his face close to the crack of the door. Tom was touched, for he knew by his own experience how this wretch had suffered. But nevertheless he felt an abounding sense of relief and security now. Injun Joe was buried near the mouth of the cave. The morning after the funeral Tom took Huck to a private place to have an important talk.

"Huck, that money wasn't ever in No. 2! It's in the cave! Will you go in there with me and help get it out?"

"I bet I will! I will if it's where we can blaze our way to it and not get lost."

A trifle after noon the boys borrowed a small skiff from a citizen who was absent, and got under way at once. When they were several miles below Cave Hollow, Tom said: "Now, Huck, where we're a-standing you could touch that hole I got out of with a fishing-pole. Here you are! Look at it, Huck; it's the snuggest hole in this country. You just keep mum about it. All along I've been wanting to be a robber but I knew I'd got to have a thing like this, and where to run across it was the bother."

By this time everything was ready and the boys entered the hole, Tom in the lead. They toiled their way to the farther end of the tunnel, then made their spliced kite strings fast and moved on. Tom whispered:

"Now I'll show you something, Huck."

He held his candle aloft and said:

"Look as far around the corner as you can. Do you see that? There, on the big rock over yonder, done with candle smoke."

"Tom, it's a cross!"

"Now where's your No. 2? 'Under the cross,' hey? Right yonder's where I saw Injun Joe poke up his candle, Huck!"

Tom went first, cutting rude steps in the clay hill as he descended. Huck followed.

"Looky here, Huck, there's footprints and some candle-grease on the clay about one side of this rock, but not on the other sides. I'm going to dig in the clay."

"That ain't no bad notion, Tom!" said Huck with animation.

Tom had not dug four inches before he struck wood.

"My goodness, Huck, looky here!"

It was the treasure box, sure enough, occupying a snug little cavern.

"Got it at last!" said Huck, ploughing among the tarnished coins with his hands. "My, but we're rich, Tom!"

"Huck, I always reckoned we'd get it. It's just too good to believe, but we have

got it, sure! Say, let's not fool around here. I reckon I was right to think of fetching the little bags along."

The money was soon in the bags and the boys took it up to the cross rock.

"Come along, Huck, we've been in here a long time. It's getting late, I reckon. I'm hungry, too. We'll hide the money in the loft of the widow's woodshed, and I'll come up in the morning and we'll count and divide. Just you

lay quiet here and watch the stuff till I run and hook Benny Taylor's little wagon; I won't be gone a minute."

He disappeared, and presently returned with the wagon. When the boys reached the Welshman's house, they stopped to rest. Just as they were about to move on, the Welshman stepped out and said:

"Hallo, who's that?"

"Huck and Tom Sawyer."

"Good! Come along with me, boys, you are keeping everybody waiting. Here, hurry up, trot ahead, I'll haul the wagon for you. Why, it's not as light as it might be. Got bricks in it, or old metal?"

"Old metal," said Tom.

"Hurry along, hurry along!"

The boys wanted to know what the hurry was about.

"Never mind; you'll see, when we get to the Widow Douglas's."

Huck's found himself pushed, along with Tom, into Mrs. Douglas's drawing-room. The place was grandly lighted, and everybody that was of any consequence in the village was there. Mr. Jones said:

"Tom wasn't at home, yet, so I gave him up; but I stumbled on him and Huck right at my door, and so I just brought them along in a hurry."

"And you did just right," said the widow. "Come with me, boys."

Some minutes later the widow's guests were at the supper table, and a dozen children were propped up at little side tables in the same room, after the fashion of that country and day.

The widow said she meant to give Huck a home under her roof and have him educated; and that when she could spare the money she would start him in business in a modest way. Tom's chance was come. He said:

"Huck don't need it. Huck's rich."

The silence was a little awkward. Tom broke it:

"Huck's got money. Maybe you don't believe it, but he's got lots of it. Oh, you needn't smile, I reckon I can show you. You just wait a minute."

Tom ran out of doors. The company looked at each other with a perplexed interest, and inquiringly at Huck, who was tongue-tied.

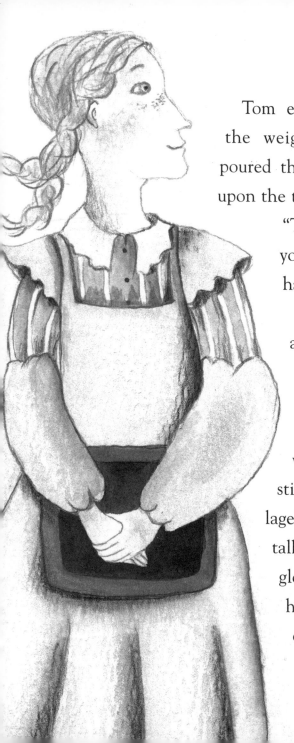

Tom entered, struggling with the weight of his sacks, and poured the mass of yellow coins upon the table and said:

"There, what did I tell you? Half of it's Huck's and half of it's mine!"

Then there was a unanimous call for an explanation. Tom said he could furnish it, and he did.

Tom and Huck's windfall made a mighty stir in the poor little village of St. Petersburg. It was talked about, gloated over, glorified. Judge Thatcher had conceived a great opinion of Tom. He said that no commonplace boy would ever have got his daughter out of the cave. When Becky told her father, in strict confidence, how Tom had taken her whipping at school, the Judge was visibly moved; he said he meant to look to it that Tom should be admitted to the National Military Academy and afterwards trained in the best law school in the country, in order that he might be ready for either career or both.

About the Author

Samuel Clemens was born on November 30, 1835 in Florida, Missouri. When he was four years old, his family moved to Hannibal, Missouri, which became his childhood home and the inspiration for many of his stories. He eventually took on the pen name of Mark Twain, and had his first short story published in 1865. His first book, *The Innocents Abroad*, was published in 1869. Twain wrote many stories and novels but he is best remembered for *The Adventures of Tom Sawyer* and *The Adventures of Huckleberry Finn*. His works were popular during his lifetime, and brought him close to artists, royalty, and presidents. Today, Mark Twain is regarded as one of America's greatest and best-loved authors.

KING ARTHUR
AND THE KNIGHTS OF THE ROUND TABLE

Benedict Flynn

Read by Sean Bean

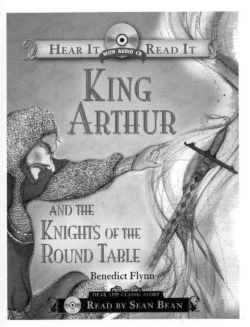

In *King Arthur and the Knights of the Round Table*, young Arthur is as surprised as anyone the day he pulls the mysterious sword from the stone and becomes the king of England! The wizard Merlin leads him to assemble his knights, including brave Sir Lancelot and pure Sir Galahad. Arthur and his knights undertake many quests to bring peace to the kingdom, and uphold justice for all. But all the while, the evil Morgana le Fay and Mordred plot to overthrow Arthur and rule themselves. Soon Arthur enters a terrible battle . . . for his kingdom, and his life.

$9.95 U.S/$11.95 CAN/£6.99 UK   ISBN-13: 978-1-4022-1243-7
ISBN-10: 1-4022-1243-7